Mop's Backyard Concert

by Martine Schaap and Alex de Wolf

Cricket/McGraw-Hill

"Mop and Family" appears monthly in *Ladybug*® magazine.
Visit our Web site at www.ladybugmag.com or call 1-800-827-0227
or write to *Ladybug* magazine, 315 Fifth Street, Peru, IL 61354.

Send all inquiries to:
McGraw-Hill Consumer Products
8787 Orion Place
Columbus, OH 43240-4027

1-57768-892-9

1 2 3 4 5 6 7 8 9 10 RRD-W 05 04 03 02 01 00

Library of Congress Cataloging-in-Publication Data

Schaap, Martine.
    Mop's backyard concert / by Martine Schaap and Alex de Wolf.
       p. cm.
    Summary: After their sheepdog Mop runs away at the park to join a group of outdoor musicians, twins Julie and Justin are inspired to create their own band. Includes instructions for making simple musical instruments.
       ISBN 1-57768-892-9
    [1. Dogs--Fiction. 2. Bands (Music)--Fiction.]   I. Wolf, Alex de.
II. Title.
    PZ7.S32775 Mp 2000
    [E]--dc21
                                                                          00-010030

"Listen!" said Julie. A faint *ting-a-ling* was coming from the park.

"My favorite music!" said Justin. "Can we see where it's coming from?"

"Please, Dad, please?" said the twins together.

The cheerful tinkling led them right to an ice cream stand. "Okay, what flavors do you want?" asked Dad.

"I want banana," said Justin. "Please."

"Strawberry for me," said Julie. "Thanks, Dad!"

"And I'd like—"
But before Dad could order his own ice cream cone,
Julie cried, "Where's Mop?"

"Oh no, I must have dropped the leash!" said Julie.
"There's something rustling in those bushes. Maybe
it's Mop!" said Justin. He and Julie started to run. Dad
followed them.

When they got to the bushes, a squirrel jumped out
and scampered away.

"That's not Mop!" said Justin.

"Oh, poor Mop, he's lost," Julie said. "He'll be so scared!"

"Mop! Here, Mop!" The twins called and called as they ran along the park path. No shaggy sheepdog answered their call.

Then they heard a new sound. Julie stopped running to listen. "Is that a drum?" she asked.

"Yes," said Justin, "but what's that other noise?"

A weird howling broke off in a familiar bark! Justin and Julie looked at each other. "Mop!" they exclaimed and started to run again, with Dad still trailing behind them.

"There you are, Mop!" Julie hugged their big shaggy dog. "We thought you were lost!"

Justin picked up the leash and handed it to Dad. "Don't run away like that again, Mop," he said. "You worried us!"

"Is that your dog?" asked the trumpet player. "He has quite a voice."

"He's been singing along with us," added the trombone player.

Wham, bang! The drum boomed. Cymbals clanged.
People stopped to listen as the band started to play again.
A xylophone chimed a cheery melody, and the trumpet
and clarinet sang in harmony.

The oompah tuba rumbled the bass line, while the slide trombone moaned in between. People clapped in time, and some of them hummed along. Julie and Justin clapped with the crowd, and Mop howled once or twice, until Dad made him stop.

When the music was finished, the crowd clapped
loudly. The trombone player passed his cap, and everyone
put money in it.

On the way home, Dad whistled one of the tunes they had just heard.

"That was fun," said Julie. "I liked the drums."

"Me, too," said Justin. "Hey, we can make our own band!"

"Great idea!" said Julie.

As soon as they got home, Julie and Justin headed for the kitchen.

"These pan lids will be my cymbals," said Justin.

"And this pot will make a great drum," Julie said.

Dad peeked around the kitchen door and said,
"Sounds like fun. Can I play, too?"
"Sure, Dad," said Julie, "join the band!"
"What are you going to play?" asked Justin.

"I have an idea," said Dad. "Justin, will you get me two spoons from the drawer? And Julie, hand me some water glasses, please."

Dad poured water into the glasses.

"I'm making a water xylophone," he explained. "The different levels of water make the sound higher or lower." He tapped the glasses with the spoons. Julie banged her drum, and Justin clanged his cymbals. *Clink-clink! Bang! Clang!*

"Now we're just like the band in the park," Justin said.

"Almost," said Julie. "But we need an audience!"

17

Julie and Justin invited Mom,
Granddad,

their neighbor,
and their friends, Sarah
and Dan.

"The concert will be outside," said Julie. "Just like the one we heard in the park."

Julie and Justin set up chairs. Dad put his water glasses on the picnic table.

Just then Granddad arrived. "Aha, refreshments!" he said, reaching for a glass.

"Refreshments are after the concert," Justin told him. "That's Dad's water xylophone."

Concert time! The audience scurried to their seats.
Justin set a beat with his cymbals. *CLANG, two, three,
four, CLANG, two, three, four.* Everyone clapped in time
and tapped their feet.

Julie drummed. *Thump, thump-a-thump, thump.*
Thump, thump-a-thump, thump. Dad clinked his glasses,
and Mom hummed along. Mop pointed his nose in the
air and began to yowl. *Woooo! Woooo!*

Everyone stopped and stared at him. Mop wagged his
tail. Then he put his big front feet up on the picnic table
and shoved his nose into the water xylophone. The glasses
tipped. Water spilled everywhere!

"Mop, stop!" cried Justin.

"He must be thirsty," said Julie.

"From all his singing," added Justin.

"We have lemonade for everyone," said Dad. "And I'll get a big bowl of water for our poor, dry singer."

"Dry? He doesn't look dry to me!" exclaimed Julie.

Just then Mop shook himself. Water flew everywhere! Justin started to laugh. "We should play, 'It's Raining, It's Pouring!'"

Julie laughed, too. "Or, 'Rain, Rain, Go Away!'" she said.

"Just so Mop doesn't go away," said Justin. "We don't want him to get lost again."

"But everything turned out okay," added Julie. "If Mop hadn't gotten lost, we wouldn't have found the band in the park."

"You're right, Julie," replied Justin. "And we have something that band doesn't have . . . a singing Mop!"

Backyard Concert Activities

Bells

Thread three or four large jingle bells onto a pipe cleaner and shape it into a circle large enough to fit over your hand. Twist the ends of the pipe cleaner together and slip the circle on like a bracelet. Shake your hand as you dance!

Cymbals

Two metal pan lids make a great pair of cymbals.

Oatmeal Box Drum

Cut a piece of finger-painting paper or glossy shelf paper to a size that fits around the outside of a large, round cardboard carton (such as an oatmeal box). Put the piece of paper on a flat surface to finger paint a design on it. When the paint is dry, glue the paper to the carton. Drum on the carton lid with your hands or with wooden spoons.

Comb Kazoo

Fold a piece of tissue paper over a comb. Hold it flat against your lips and sing a melody, making an "ooo" sound. Experiment to figure out how tightly you need to press the comb against your upper lip to get the most vibration.

Kazoo Bugle

Place a square of waxed paper over the end of a cardboard tube (such as a paper towel or toilet paper tube) and secure it with a rubber band. Sing a "wooo-wooo" tune into the open end of the tube, experimenting with how tightly you need to press the tube against your mouth for the most vibration. You can also turn the tube around and sing against the waxed paper for a different effect.

Maracas

Put a spoonful or two of dried beans or rice into each of two paper cups. Turn two empty paper cups upside-down over the first ones and tape each pair together with masking tape. Mix some school glue with an equal amount of water in a shallow pan or plate. Tear strips of construction paper, dip them in the watery glue, and paste them to the cups. Cover the cups completely with colorful paper strips. When the glue is dry, shake the maracas in a lively musical beat.

Rhythm Sticks

Tap two wooden spoons together in time to the music.

Kettle Drum

Turn a large cooking kettle upside-down and use the bottom as a drum. Experiment with different kinds of drumsticks: wooden spoons are great. Try brushing the kettle with a wire whisk for an unusual-sounding drumbeat.